The Cat Wh
Loved

Once there was a cat
who loved red.

She loved to eat from a red dish.

She loved to play with a ball of red yarn.

She loved to chase
a red bird.

She loved to wear a red bell
on her red collar.

She loved to sleep
on a red pillow.

But most of all, she loved the girl with red hair.